Books by Raymond Briggs:

Jim and the Beanstalk
The Elephant and the Bad Baby
The Mother Goose Treasury
The Fairy Tale Treasury
Father Christmas
Father Christmas Goes on Holiday
Fungus the Bogeyman
The Snowman
The Snowman Pop-Up
Gentleman Jim
When the Wind Blows
The Fungus the Bogeyman Plop-Up Book
The Tin Pot Foreign General and the Old Iron Woman

FATHER CHRISTMAS

RAYMOND BRIGGS
Father Christmas

HAMISH HAMILTON
London

For my Mother and Father

© 1973 Raymond Briggs
All rights reserved
First published in Great Britain 1973 by
Hamish Hamilton Children's Books
27 Wright's Lane, London W8 5TZ

Reprinted 1973, 1974, 1976, 1977, 1978, 1980, 1982, 1983, 1985, 1986.
ISBN 0 241 02260 6

Printed and bound in Spain by A. G. Elkar, S. Coop.-Bilbao

Father Christmas

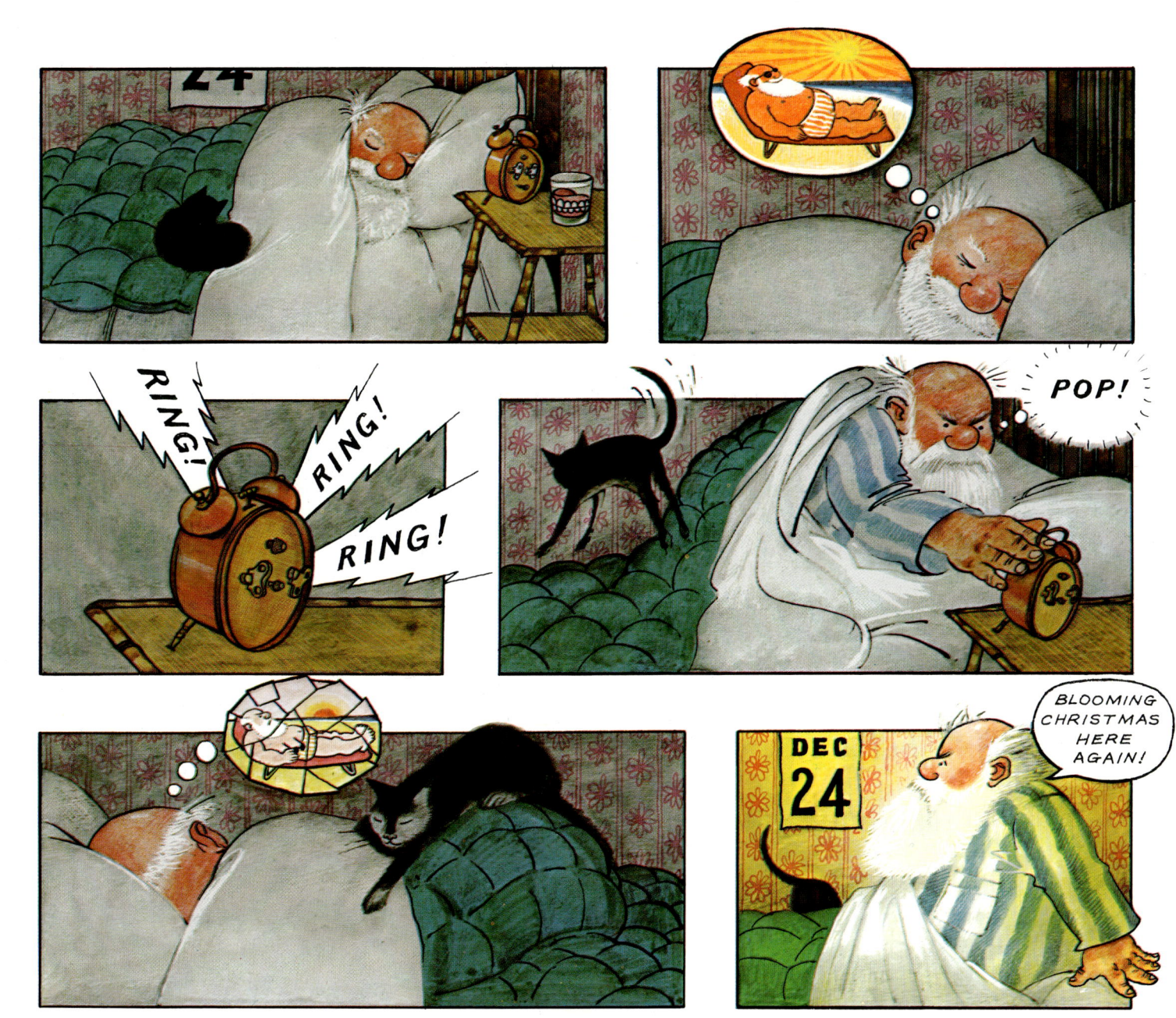

"HM, BETTER THAN NOTHING I SUPPOSE."

WHOA!

The End